RAINBOW magic

RAINBOW FAIRIES

HEATHER
THE VIOLET FAIRY

By Daisy Meadows
Illustrated by Georgie Ripper

Silver Dolphin

Silver Dolphin

Silver Dolphin Books
An imprint of Printers Row Publishing Group
A division of Readerlink Distribution Services, LLC
9717 Pacific Heights Blvd, San Diego, CA 92121
www.silverdolphinbooks.com

Printers Row Publishing Group is a division of
Readerlink Distribution Services, LLC.
Silver Dolphin Books is a registered trademark of
Readerlink Distribution Services, LLC.

All notations of errors or omissions should be addressed to Silver Dolphin Books, Editorial Department, at the above address. All other correspondence (author inquiries, permissions) concerning the content of this book should be addressed to:
Hachette Children's Group
Carmelite House
50 Victoria Embankment
London
EC4Y 0DZ

ISBN: 978-1-6672-0440-6
Manufactured, printed, and assembled in Guangzhou, China.
First printing, May 2023. GD/05/23
27 26 25 24 23   1 2 3 4 5

HEATHER
THE VIOLET FAIRY

The Fairyland Palace

Maze

Forest

Orchard

Black Pot

Meadow

Tower

Beach

Tide pools

Rainspell Island

Shel

Jack Frost's Ice Castle

Tom Goodfellow's House

Merry-go-round

Willow Tree

Mrs. Merry's Cottage

Stream

Field

Mermaid Cottage

Town

Harbor

Dolphin Cottage

COLD WINDS BLOW AND THICK ICE FORM,
I CONJURE UP THIS FAIRY STORM.
TO SEVEN CORNERS OF THE HUMAN WORLD
THE RAINBOW FAIRIES WILL BE HURLED!

I CURSE EVERY PART OF FAIRYLAND,
WITH A FROSTY WAVE OF MY ICY HAND.
FOR NOW AND ALWAYS, FROM THIS DAY,
FAIRYLAND WILL BE COLD AND GRAY!

Rachel and Kirsty have found all the Rainbow Fairies except one. But the fairies will never get their Rainbow Magic back without

HEATHER THE VIOLET FAIRY!

Table of Contents

MESSAGE ON A KITE

"I can't believe this is the last day of our vacation on Rainspell Island!" said Rachel Walker. She gazed up at her kite as it flew through the clear blue sky.

Kirsty Tate watched the purple kite soar above the field beside Mermaid Cottage. "But we still have to find Heather!" she reminded Rachel.

Jack Frost had cast a wicked spell that banished the seven Rainbow Fairies to Rainspell Island. And without the Rainbow Fairies, Fairyland had lost all of its color! The Fairy King and Queen had asked Kirsty and Rachel to help find the fairies. The girls had already found Ruby, Amber, Sunny, Fern, Sky, and Inky. Now they only had Heather the Violet Fairy left to find.

Rachel felt a tug on the kite's string. She looked up. Something violet and silver flashed at the end of the kite's long tail. "Look up there!" she shouted.

Kirsty shaded her eyes with her hand. "What is it? Do you think it's a fairy?" she asked.

"I'm not sure," Rachel said, pulling in the string.

As the kite floated toward them, Kirsty saw that a long piece of violet-colored ribbon was tied to its tail. She helped Rachel untie the ribbon and smooth it out on the ground.

"It has tiny silver writing on it," Rachel said.

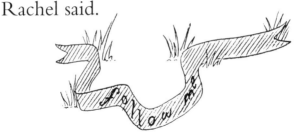

Kirsty crouched down to have a closer look. "It says, *follow me*."

Suddenly, the ribbon was swept up by the breeze. It fluttered across the field.

"It must be leading us to Heather!" Kirsty said, jumping up.

11

Rachel gathered up her kite. "Mom, is it OK if we go exploring one last time?" she called.

Mrs. Walker was talking to Kirsty's mom in the yard outside Mermaid Cottage. Kirsty's family was staying in Dolphin Cottage, right next door.

"Of course, as long as Kirsty's mom agrees," Mrs. Walker replied.

"It's fine by me," said Mrs. Tate. "But don't go far. The ferry leaves at four o'clock."

"We'll have to hurry!" Rachel whispered to Kirsty.

The girls ran through the soft, green grass, following the ribbon. It bobbed and drifted on the breeze.

Suddenly, the ribbon flew out of sight behind a thick hedge.

"Where did it go?" Kirsty wondered.

"Through here!" Rachel said, pulling back one of the branches.

13

Kirsty followed her friend through the
hedge. Luckily, the leaves weren't too
prickly. On the other side, they found
a path and a gate. There was a sign
on the gate, in purple paint, that read:
SUMMER FAIR TODAY!

Kirsty and Rachel went through the gate and into a pretty garden. There were stalls full of cotton candy and ice cream at the edge of a smooth, green lawn. There were people everywhere, chatting and laughing.

"Isn't this great?" Rachel said, looking around in surprise. A woman with a little girl holding a bunch of balloons smiled at her.

Suddenly, Kirsty spotted the ribbon
fluttering toward a merry-go-round at
the far end of the lawn. It wrapped itself
around the golden flagpole and danced in
the breeze like a tiny flag.

"It must be leading us to
the merry-go-round!"
Kirsty said. She grabbed
her friend's hand and
they ran across the
grass together.
The merry-
go-round was as
pretty as a fairy
castle. Rachel
stared at the circle
of wooden horses on
their shiny golden poles.
They were beautiful!

"Hello there!" called a friendly voice behind them. "I'm Tom Goodfellow. Do you like my merry-go-round?"

Rachel and Kirsty turned to see an old man with white hair and a kind smile. "Yes, it's wonderful," Rachel said.

Kirsty watched the wooden horses rising and falling in time to the cheerful music. "Look, Rachel." She gasped. "The horses are all painted in rainbow colors! Red, orange, yellow, green, blue, indigo, and violet."

Rachel looked more closely. Through the spinning horses, she could see that the pillar in the center of the merry-go-round was decorated with a picture of rainbow-colored horses galloping along a beach.

Just then, the merry-go-round slowed down and the music stopped. Mr. Goodfellow climbed up to help the riders off their horses. "All aboard for the next ride!" he called. More excited children began to climb up onto the horses.

Mr. Goodfellow smiled down at Rachel and Kirsty. "How about you two?" he asked, his blue eyes twinkling.

A MAGICAL RIDE

"We'd love to take a ride on your merry-go-round!" said Kirsty. "Quick, Rachel, there are two horses left!" She scrambled up onto one of them. A name was painted in gold on the saddle. "My horse is named Indigo Princess," Kirsty said, stroking the horse's shiny coat.

Rachel climbed onto a pretty horse

next to Kirsty's. It had a lilac-colored coat and a silver mane. "Mine is named Prancing Violet."

"Hold on, everyone!" Mr. Goodfellow called out.

The music started and the merry-go-round began to turn. Prancing Violet and Indigo Princess swooped up and down on their painted poles.

22

Rachel laughed out loud as the merry-go-round spun faster and faster. The garden flashed by, and the flowers and paths disappeared in a blur. The sounds of music and laughter faded away. Rachel's heart skipped a beat. Now, the only horse she could see was Kirsty's horse, Indigo Princess. Suddenly, she could feel Prancing Violet's hooves thudding on the ground beneath her.

Kirsty felt a sea breeze whirling through her hair. Indigo Princess seemed to toss her head and kick up sand as she galloped along.

"Wow!" Kirsty exclaimed, tasting salt spray on her lips. "This is like riding a real horse!"

"It's awesome!" Rachel agreed. She felt as if they were racing along a beach, just like the horses she'd seen in the painting on the merry-go-round.

But before Rachel could say anything else, the horses began to slow down. The sandy beach faded away, and the sound of music returned. The merry-go-round came to a smooth stop.

Kirsty patted Indigo Princess's neck as she dismounted. "Thanks for the special ride!" she whispered. Then she turned to Rachel. "This merry-go-round is definitely magical, but where is Heather the Violet Fairy?"

Rachel slipped off of Prancing Violet's saddle and frowned. "I don't know," she said. Then she heard a tiny laugh coming from behind her. Rachel turned around. There was nobody there, just the picture on the pillar in the middle of the merry-go-round.

Rachel blinked. There was a fairy riding the violet-colored horse! She wore a purple dress, high purple knee socks, and ballet slippers. A few purple flowers were tucked behind one of her ears.

"Kirsty!" Rachel whispered, pointing. "I think I just found Heather the Violet Fairy!"

25

THE SEVENTH FAIRY

Mr. Goodfellow was still helping the other riders off the horses. Quickly, Rachel and Kirsty squeezed past the other horses to look more closely at the pillar.

"Heather must be trapped in the painting!" Rachel said.

"We have to get her out!" Kirsty said.

"Yes," Rachel agreed. "But what can we do with all these people around?"

Just then, almost as if he had heard them, Mr. Goodfellow clapped his hands. "Follow me, everyone. The clowns are here!"

Everyone cheered as they ran across the lawn toward the clowns. Rachel and Kirsty were left alone.

"Now's our chance!" Kirsty said.

Rachel had an idea. "I know! Let's use

our magic bags," she said. Titania, the
Fairy Queen, had given Kirsty and
Rachel bags of special gifts to help them
rescue the Rainbow Fairies.

"Of course! I have mine here." Kirsty
put her hand in her pocket and took
out her magic bag. It was
glowing with a soft,
golden light. When she
opened it, a cloud of
glitter fizzed up into
the air.

Kirsty slipped
her hand into the
bag. There was
something inside,
long and skinny like
a pencil. It was a tiny
golden paintbrush.

Kirsty was confused. "What good is that? We don't want to paint any *more* pictures."

"Maybe Heather knows what we can use it for," Rachel suggested. "Amber told us how to help her when she was trapped in the shell, remember?"

"Good idea," Kirsty said. As she bent closer to the pillar, the tip of the brush touched the painted fairy's hand.

Suddenly, the whole picture glowed, and the fairy's tiny fingers moved! A single violet-scented petal floated down from the picture.

"Look!" Rachel gasped.

"The brush is working some magic on the painting!" Kirsty whispered.

She began to stroke the brush all
around the outline of the fairy.

At first, nothing seemed to happen.
Then the picture glowed even brighter.
The fairy shivered. "That tickles!" she
said with a tiny laugh.

The magic brush was lifting Heather
out of the painting!

Rachel checked to make sure
that no one was watching
them. Then, with Kirsty's
last stroke, the fairy
sprang out of the
painting, her wings
flashing like jewels.
Purple fairy dust shot
everywhere, turning into
violet-scented blossoms
that floated around her.

"Thank you so much for rescuing me!" said Heather, floating in front of them. She held a purple wand, tipped with silver. "I'm Heather the Violet Fairy! Who are you? Do you know where my Rainbow sisters are?"

"I'm Rachel, and this is Kirsty," said Rachel. "Your sisters are all safe in the pot at the end of the rainbow."

"Hooray!" Heather did a twirl of excitement, scattering violet sparks around the girls. "I can't wait to see them again."

Kirsty held out her hand and Heather landed gently on it.

Kirsty hid her from view until they had run through the garden, past all the people watching the clowns. They ran out of the gate and down the path that led to the woods. Deep inside the woods was a peaceful clearing with a willow tree on one side. The pot at the end of the rainbow was hidden under its long branches.

As soon as Rachel and Kirsty reached the clearing, there was a shout from inside the pot. Inky the Indigo Fairy zoomed out. "Heather! You're safe!" she cried. "Look, everybody! Rachel and Kirsty have found our missing sister!"

The other Rainbow Fairies were close behind Inky. Sunny even flew out of the pot on the back of a huge bumblebee! The air flashed and fizzed with scented bubbles, flowers, leaves, stars, ink drops, and tiny butterflies. Bertram the frog

hopped out from behind the pot, with a huge smile on his broad, green face.

As the fairies flew up to hug and kiss Heather, her blossom-filled fairy dust mingled with theirs, and the smell of violets filled the clearing.

"We *knew* you were coming," said Amber the Orange Fairy, doing a cartwheel in the air. "I've been feeling extra magical all morning!"

35

Rachel and Kirsty held hands and danced in a circle. They'd done it! They had found all seven Rainbow Fairies!

"And who is this?" Heather asked Sunny the Yellow Fairy, reaching out to tickle the queen bee under her chin.

"This is Queenie," said Sunny, kissing the bee's furry head. "She rescued my wand after the goblins stole it."

Ruby the Red
Fairy's wings
sparkled as she
fluttered down
and landed on
Rachel's shoulder.
"Thank you,
Rachel and
Kirsty," she said.

"You are true fairy
friends," added Fern the
Green Fairy, drifting
onto Kirsty's hand.
"And now that we're all
together again, we must
use our magic to make a
rainbow to take us back
to Fairyland."

Suddenly, Rachel heard a strange crackling sound. She spun around. The pond at the edge of the clearing wasn't blue anymore. It was white and cloudy with ice! Rachel and Kirsty and the fairies looked at one another in alarm.

"Goblins!" they whispered. Sky the Blue Fairy shivered with fright and fluttered closer to Sunny and Queenie for protection.

Inky's tiny teeth chattered. "B-b-but it can't be. The Sugarplum Fairy kept them in the Land of Sweets, picking jelly beans!"

Just then, a harsh, cackling laugh rang out. The bushes parted, and a tall, bony figure walked into the clearing. Icicles hung from his clothes, and there was frost on his white hair and eyebrows.

It was Jack Frost!

FAIRY SPELLS

"So, you are all together again!" Jack Frost cackled. His angry voice sounded like icicles snapping in half.

"Yes, thanks to Rachel and Kirsty," Ruby answered bravely. "And now we want to go home to Fairyland!"

Jack Frost gave a laugh like hailstones cracking against a window.

"I will never allow that!" he told them. But before Jack Frost could do anything, Ruby the Red Fairy flew high into the air.

"Come on, Rainbow Fairies! Now that we're together again, all of our Rainbow Magic has come back. This time, we must try to stop Jack Frost with a spell. Follow me!" she called.

Immediately, Inky shot to her sister's side and turned to face Jack Frost with her hands on her hips and a determined look on her face. The other fairy sisters flew to join them, and they all lifted their wands, chanting together:

42

To protect the Rainbow Fairies all,
Make a magic raindrop wall!

Kirsty held Rachel's hand and watched, feeling very scared. Would the spell work?

A rainbow-colored spray shot out of each wand and a shining wall of raindrops appeared. It hung like a waterfall between the fairies and Jack Frost.

Rachel and Kirsty both held their breath.

"It will take more than a few raindrops to stop me!" Jack Frost hissed. He pointed one bony finger at the shimmering wall.

At once, the raindrops turned to ice. They dropped onto the frosty grass, like tiny glass beads, and shattered.

All the fairies looked horrified. Sunny
and Sky gave cries of dismay, and Inky
clenched her fists. Fern, Amber, and
Ruby hugged one another tightly.
Heather hovered off to one side, looking
like she was thinking hard.

Rachel and Kirsty stared in alarm as Jack Frost lifted his hand again.

Then Heather flew forward, waved her wand, and cried:

*To stop Jack Frost
from causing trouble,
Catch him in a magic bubble!*

A gleaming bubble popped out of the end of Heather's wand. It grew bigger and bigger. It looked like it was made of pale lilac glass.

Jack Frost started to laugh, and stretched out his icy fingers. But before he could do anything else, there was a loud fizzing sound. Jack Frost disappeared!

Rachel blinked.

Heather's spell had trapped Jack Frost *inside* the bubble! It bobbed gently down onto the grass. Jack Frost pressed his hands against the shiny wall and looked furious.

"Great job, Heather!" Fern exclaimed.

"Quick, everyone. We have to get
into the pot and make a magic rainbow
to take us back to Fairyland!" Heather
urged. "Jack Frost could still escape!"

Rachel and Kirsty held the branches of
the willow tree out of the way so that
the fairies could fly through.

48

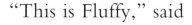

Heather's tiny eyebrows shot up as a squirrel scampered down the willow tree's trunk, toward the pot. "Who are you?" she asked.

"This is Fluffy," said Fern, stroking the squirrel. "He helped me escape from the goblins."

"Fluffy and Queenie will have to go back to their homes now," said Sky sadly.

"Can't they live with you in Fairyland?" Rachel asked.

"No, their homes are here, on Rainspell Island," Fern explained. "But we'll come and visit them, won't we?" All the fairies nodded and Sunny wiped away a tiny tear.

Fern reached up to give Fluffy one
last hug. Her sisters fluttered around,
saying good-bye to Queenie and Fluffy.

"Thank you again for all your help,"
said Ruby.

Queenie buzzed good-bye as she flew
away. Fluffy gave a farewell flick of his
tail, then scampered off.

50

Heather fluttered in front of Rachel and Kirsty. "Would you like to come to Fairyland with us? I'm sure Queen Titania and King Oberon will want to thank you."

Rachel and Kirsty nodded eagerly. Heather smiled and waved her wand, sprinkling the girls with purple fairy dust.

Kirsty felt herself shrinking. The grass seemed to rush toward her. "Hooray! I'm a fairy again!" she cried.

Rachel laughed as wings sprang from her shoulders.

Just then, there was a yell from inside the giant bubble.

Rachel and Kirsty looked around. Jack Frost was looking very scared. His face was bright red, and drops of water ran down his cheeks. He was *melting*!

"Well, he can't stop you from getting to Fairyland now," said Kirsty.

But Sky's wings drooped. She hovered in the air, looking sad.

"Without Jack Frost, there will be no seasons," she pointed out. "We need his cold and ice to make winter."

"No winter?" Inky said, looking shocked. "But I love sledding in the snow and skating on the frozen river."

"Without winter, when will we have spring?"Amber said in a small voice. "What will happen to all the beautiful spring flowers?"

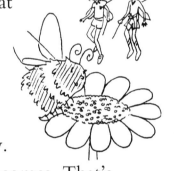

"And the bees need the flowers to make honey in summer," Sunny said sadly.

"After summer, autumn comes. That's when squirrels find nuts to store for hibernation," said Fern. "We need all the seasons, you see. If we leave Jack Frost in that bubble . . ."

The fairies looked upset. Then Heather
spoke up. "This is all true. But I also
feel sorry for Jack Frost. He looks very
frightened."

"Heather's right. We have to do
something," said Ruby.

"But he might cast another spell!"
Kirsty said.

"Even so, we have to help him, don't
we?" Amber said firmly. All the other
Rainbow Fairies agreed.

Kirsty felt so proud of them. The fairies
were being so kind and brave.

"I know what to do!" Sky flew
over the giant bubble. She looked
nervous, being so close to Jack
Frost, and she whispered her
spell so quietly that Rachel
and Kirsty couldn't hear the words.

54

A jet of blue fairy dust streamed out of Sky's wand and into the bubble. The dust swirled in a spiral, bigger and bigger, until it filled the whole bubble.

Rachel and Kirsty flew over and peered in.

The fairy dust had turned into huge crystal snowflakes. The water on Jack Frost's face froze into tiny drops of ice. He had stopped melting! The wind spun the snow faster, whirling around Jack Frost in circles.

"Look! He's getting smaller and smaller!" Kirsty gasped.

55

She was right. First Jack Frost
was smaller than a goblin. Then he was
smaller than a squirrel, then even smaller
than Queenie the bee. Everyone looked
from the bubble to Sky and back again.
What was going to happen next?

With a loud *POP*, the bubble
burst. The wind stopped and the
snow vanished.

At first, Kirsty
thought Jack Frost
had completely
disappeared. Then
she noticed a very
small glass globe
lying on the grass.
Inside the globe,
a tiny figure leaped
around angrily.

"It's a snow globe!" Kirsty said in amazement. "And Jack Frost is trapped inside!"

TIME FOR A RAINBOW

"Hooray for Sky!" shouted Rachel.
"Now Jack Frost can't hurt any of us,
and we can take him safely back to
Fairyland." Rachel flew over and picked
up the snow globe. It felt smooth and
cold, and it trembled when Jack Frost
jumped around inside.

Bertram hopped toward Rachel. "I'll take care of that, Miss Rachel," he said.

Rachel was glad to hand over the snow globe. She didn't like being so close to Jack Frost!

"Into the pot, everybody!" shouted Inky. "It's time to go back to Fairyland!"

"Yippee!" yelled Amber, doing a backflip in midair.

Heather waved her wand and the pot rolled upright, onto its four short legs.

Rachel, Kirsty, and all the fairies flew inside. Bertram the frog climbed in after them. It was a little cramped, but Rachel

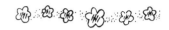

and Kirsty were too excited to care.

"Ready?" Ruby asked.

Her sisters nodded, looking very serious. The seven Rainbow Fairies raised their wands. There was a flash above them, like rainbow-colored fireworks. A fountain of sparks filled the pot with beautiful bold colors: red, orange, yellow, green, blue, indigo, and violet.

And then the brightest rainbow
Rachel and Kirsty had ever seen soared
upward into the clear blue sky.

With a *whoosh*, Bertram and the
fairies shot out of the pot, carried on
the rainbow like a giant wave. Rachel
and Kirsty felt themselves zooming up
the rainbow too. Flowers, stars, leaves,
tiny butterflies, ink drops, and bubbles
made of fairy dust fizzed and popped
around them.

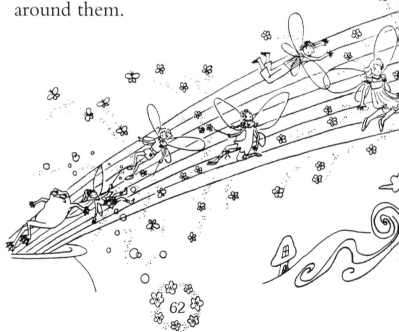

"This is amazing!" Kirsty shouted.

Far below, she could see hills dotted
with toadstool houses. It was Fairyland!
There was the winding river and the
royal palace with its four pointed towers.

All of a sudden, the rainbow vanished in a fizz of fairy dust. Kirsty and Rachel flapped their wings and drifted gently to the ground. Rachel looked around, expecting to see all the colors coming back to Fairyland.

But the hills and the toadstool houses were still gray!

"Why hasn't the color returned?" Rachel gasped in horror.

Kirsty shrugged, too worried to speak.

One by one, the Rainbow Fairies landed softly next to the girls. And Kirsty saw that where each fairy had landed on the gray grass, a patch of the greenest green was spreading outward.

"Rachel, look!" Kirsty shouted. "The grass is turning green!"

"Oh, yes!" Rachel said. Her eyes shone.

The fairy sisters stood in a circle and raised their wands. A fountain of rainbow-colored sparks shot up into the fluffy, white clouds. There was a flash of golden lightning, and it began to rain.

Rachel and Kirsty watched in delight as tiny glittering raindrops, in every color of the rainbow, pattered gently down around them. And where they fell, the color returned, flowing like shining paint across everything in Fairyland.

The toadstool houses gleamed red and white. Brightly colored flowers dotted the green hills with orange, yellow, and purple. The river was a bright, clear blue.

On the highest hill, the fairy palace shone softly pink. Music came out as the front doors of the palace slowly opened. Ruby flew down to Rachel and Kirsty.

"Hurry!" she said. "The King and Queen are waiting for us."

Rachel and Kirsty flew toward the palace with the seven fairies. Below them, Bertram hurried along with enormous leaps.

The Rainbow Fairies beamed as elves, pixies, and fairies rushed out of the palace and danced around. "Hooray, hooray, for the Rainbow Fairies," they cheered. "Hooray for Rachel and Kirsty!"

Queen Titania and King Oberon came out of the palace after them. The queen wore a silver dress and a sparkling diamond tiara. The king's coat and crown were made of gold.

"Welcome back, dear Rainbow Fairies. We have missed you," said Queen Titania, holding out her arms. "Thank you a thousand times, Rachel and Kirsty!"

67

Bertram gave a deep bow.
"This is for you, Your
Majesty," he said, giving the
snow globe to King Oberon.

"Thank you, Bertram,"
said the king. He held the
snow globe in both hands and
looked into it. "Now, Jack Frost,"
he said sternly. "If I let you out, will you
promise to stay in your icy castle and not
harm the Rainbow Fairies again?"

"Remember that winter still belongs to
you," Queen Titania reminded him.

Inside the snow globe, Jack Frost stroked
his sharp chin. "Very well," he said. "But
on one condition."

"And what is that?" asked the king.

Kirsty looked at Rachel, suddenly feeling
worried. What was he going to ask for?

"That I'm invited to the next Midsummer Ball," said Jack Frost.

Queen Titania smiled. "You will be very welcome," she said kindly.

The king tapped the snow globe and it cracked in half. Jack Frost sprang out and shot up to his full, skinny height. Snow glittered on his white hair. He snapped his fingers and a sleigh made of ice appeared next to him. Hopping onto it, he zoomed up into the sky.

All the fairies waved.

"Good-bye. We'll see you next year at the Midsummer Ball!" Sky called after him.

Jack Frost looked over his shoulder. A smile flickered across his sharp face. Then he was gone.

VERY SPECIAL GIFTS

The Fairy King and Queen smiled warmly at Rachel and Kirsty.

"Thank you, dear friends," said King Oberon. "Without you, Jack Frost's spell would never have been broken."

"You will always be welcome in Fairyland," Queen Titania told them. "And wherever you go, watch for magic. It will always find you."

To thank Rachel and Kirsty for their help, the king and queen gave them each a special locket filled with fairy dust.

The Rainbow Fairies fluttered over to say good-bye to the girls. Rachel and Kirsty hugged each one of them. They couldn't help feeling a little bit sad. They were going to miss their new friends very much.

Bertram hopped over and shook their hands. "Good-bye, Miss Rachel and Miss Kirsty. It was a pleasure to meet you," he said.

72

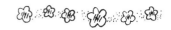

"Now here's a special rainbow to take
you home!" said Heather.

The fairy sisters raised
their wands one more
time. An enormous
rainbow whooshed
upward, stretching
all the way back to
Rainspell Island.

"Here we go!"
Rachel shouted with
joy as she felt herself
being swept up by the
glowing colors.

"I love riding on
rainbows!" cried Kirsty.

Soon Rainspell Island appeared below
them. They landed with a soft thud in
the backyard of Mermaid Cottage.

"Oh, we're back to our normal size," Rachel said, standing up.

"And we're just in time to catch the ferry!" Kirsty added as they ran around to the front yard.

"It's sad our fairy adventures are over, isn't it?" Rachel said sadly.

Kirsty nodded. "But remember what Queen Titania said about magic finding us from now on!"

"There you are," said Rachel's mom. "Did you see that beautiful rainbow? And it wasn't even raining. Rainspell Island is a really special place!"

Kirsty and Rachel shared a secret smile.

"The car's packed. Check your bedroom to see if you've left anything behind," said Kirsty's mom.

Kirsty dashed into Dolphin Cottage and went upstairs.

"I'll check mine too!" Rachel hurried into Mermaid Cottage and ran upstairs to her little attic room for the last time. She stopped in her bedroom doorway.

"Oh!" she gasped.

In the middle of the bed, something shone and glittered like a huge diamond.

Rachel walked closer. It was a snow globe, full of fluttering fairy-dust shapes in all the colors of the rainbow.

"It's the most beautiful thing I've ever seen," Rachel said. She scooped up the glass globe and dashed next door.

Kirsty was running down the stairs. She held an identical snow globe in her hands. "I'm going to keep this forever!" she said.

The two friends smiled at each other. "Every time I shake my snow globe, or see a rainbow, it will make me think of you, Fairyland, and all the Rainbow Fairies," said Rachel as they left the cottage.

"Me too!" replied Kirsty. "We'll *never* forget our secret fairy friends."

"No, we won't," said Rachel, "*Never.*"

More Titles to Read

RAINBOW FAIRIES:
RUBY THE RED FAIRY

RAINBOW FAIRIES:
AMBER THE ORANGE FAIRY

RAINBOW FAIRIES:
SUNNY THE YELLOW FAIRY

RAINBOW FAIRIES:
FERN THE GREEN FAIRY

RAINBOW FAIRIES:
SKY THE BLUE FAIRY

RAINBOW FAIRIES:
INKY THE INDIGO FAIRY

☆ ☆ ☆ ☆ ☆ ☆ ☆

BEHIND THE MAGIC

DAISY MEADOWS is a pseudonym for the four writers of the internationally best-selling *Rainbow Magic* series: Narinder Dhami, Sue Bentley, Linda Chapman, and Sue Mongredien. *Rainbow Magic* is the no.1 bestselling series for children ages 5 and up with over 40 million copies sold worldwide!

GEORGIE RIPPER was born in London and is a children's book illustrator known for her work on the *Rainbow Magic* series of fairy books. She won the Macmillan Prize for Picture Book Illustration in 2000 with *My Best Friend Bob* and *Little Brown Bushrat*, which she wrote and illustrated.